Amy* HODGEPODGE
THE SECRET'S OUT

BY KIM WAYANS & KEVIN KNOTTS
ILLUSTRATED BY SOO JEONG

Grosset & Dunlap

For Elvira, Howell, Billie, and Ivan.
And for Sylvia—the best teacher ever.

GROSSET & DUNLAP
Published by the Penguin Group
Penguin Group (USA) Inc., 375 Hudson Street, New York, New York 10014, USA
Penguin Group (Canada), 90 Eglinton Avenue East, Suite 700, Toronto, Ontario
M4P 2Y3, Canada (a division of Pearson Penguin Canada Inc.)
Penguin Books Ltd., 80 Strand, London WC2R 0RL, England
Penguin Group Ireland, 25 St. Stephen's Green, Dublin 2, Ireland
(a division of Penguin Books Ltd.)
Penguin Group (Australia), 250 Camberwell Road, Camberwell, Victoria 3124, Australia
(a division of Pearson Australia Group Pty. Ltd.)
Penguin Books India Pvt. Ltd., 11 Community Centre, Panchsheel Park,
New Delhi—110 017, India
Penguin Group (NZ), 67 Apollo Drive, Rosedale, North Shore 0632, New Zealand
(a division of Pearson New Zealand Ltd.)
Penguin Books (South Africa) (Pty.) Ltd., 24 Sturdee Avenue,
Rosebank, Johannesburg 2196, South Africa

Penguin Books Ltd., Registered Offices:
80 Strand, London WC2R 0RL, England

Copyright © 2009 Gimme Dap Productions, LLC.
Published by Grosset & Dunlap, a division of Penguin Young Readers Group,
345 Hudson Street, New York, New York 10014. GROSSET & DUNLAP is a trademark of
Penguin Group (USA) Inc. Printed in the U.S.A.

Library of Congress Control Number: 2008039467

ISBN 978-0-448-45079-7   10 9 8 7 6 5 4 3 2 1

Chapter 1

"Ugh!" Jesse groaned. "I think I just totally flunked that math quiz."

I gave her an encouraging pat on the shoulder. Jesse and I were walking down the hallway of our school, Emerson Charter, along with our three best friends: Maya, Lola, and Pia. Jesse is really smart, but she hates surprises—especially surprise quizzes. Unfortunately, she's in Mrs. Musgrove's fourth-grade class, and Mrs. Musgrove *loves* surprise quizzes! Hearing about all the quizzes she gives makes me happy to be in Mrs. Clark's class with Lola and Pia.

"That quiz *was* really hard, but I'm sure you did better than you think," Maya said as she put an arm around Jesse's shoulders. Maya's in Mrs. Musgrove's class, too.

"Anyway, look on the bright side," Maya

continued. "It's almost the weekend. That means you won't have to think about school for two whole days!"

I laughed. Maya always likes to look on the bright side!

"It's not the weekend yet," Lola reminded us. "Jesse still has to survive one more class before we even get to lunch."

"That's okay," Jesse said. "It's just art class. I don't mind *that* class at all!"

"Yeah, art class is fun," I agreed.

But secretly I was thinking that I really didn't mind *any* of my classes at Emerson. Maybe that's because I'd never gone to a real school with real classes until this year. Before that, I was homeschooled. When my family moved to Maple Heights, I asked if I could try regular school. My parents agreed, even though I could tell they were worried about how I would do. I was worried for a while, too—especially when my school year got off to a bumpy start. But it turned out that most of the kids were really nice, especially my new friends. They helped me settle in, and now I love school.

"Speaking of the weekend, I have a great idea," Lola said as we turned the corner into the hallway where the art room was located. "It's supposed to be nice and warm out tomorrow—"

"Finally!" Maya broke in with a shiver. "I thought spring would never get here!"

"Anyway," Lola went on, "I thought we could hang out at the tree house."

Lola's tree house is amazing. Her dad is an architect, and he built it for Lola and her twin brother, Cole. Then their mom helped them decorate it—she's an amazing artist. The tree house is huge, with real windows, doors, and a slanted roof.

"Great idea!" I clapped my hands. "I can bring some cookies—my Obaasan baked some last night." "Obaasan" is the Japanese word for "grandmother." That's what I call my mom's mom, who was born in Japan. She and my grandfather live with me and my parents—and my dog, Giggles.

"Yum. Your grandma's cookies are awesome, Amy!" said Jesse. Then she licked her lips.

Lola nodded. "Hey, Pia, you should help me mix up some of that pink lemonade you and I made last week. That would go great with the cookies."

Pia didn't answer. She was staring straight at the floor as she walked. Her forehead was creased beneath her stylish bangs as if she was thinking really hard about something.

"Pia?" said Jesse as she waved one hand in front of Pia's face. "Earth to Pia!"

Pia blinked her beautiful almond-shaped eyes, then frowned at Jesse. "Stop that," she said, pushing Jesse's hand away. "What are you doing?"

"We were talking about hanging at the tree house tomorrow," Lola told her. "Are you in?"

Pia shrugged. "I guess."

I exchanged a surprised glance with my friends. Pia didn't sound very excited about our weekend plans. That wasn't like her. It also wasn't like her to be so rude. Actually, now that I thought about it, Pia had been in a bad mood the previous day, too.

I thought that maybe she was just tired from her visit with her dad on Wednesday night. Her mom and dad are divorced, and her dad lives just outside of town. But when I thought about it some more, I realized it would be pretty weird for Pia to still be tired two days later.

When we reached the art room, I shrugged off the way Pia was acting. I was sure there was a simple explanation—even if I didn't know what it was.

The two fourth-grade classes are separate for most subjects, but we're all together for art, music, and gym. Art is one of my favorite classes. I always loved when I got to do arts and crafts projects for homeschooling. Plus, there's my favorite hobby—scrapbooking. It's tons of fun choosing the perfect photos for each page, decorating the margins with cute drawings or cutouts, and carefully hand-lettering all the captions. Obaasan says my scrapbook is a work of art!

Emerson's art teacher, Miss Norton, would probably agree if she ever saw it. She's really nice and always makes class interesting.

Today she was waiting to start class when we entered. We didn't even have a chance to say hi to our other friends Cole and Rusty before the teacher called for attention.

"I have some very exciting news for you," Miss Norton said, a big smile lighting up her face. "Emerson's Annual Spring Art Show is just around the corner!"

Chapter 2

"Wow, cool!" Stanley Hermann called out.

"No wonder Stanley's excited," Jesse whispered to me. "He's the best artist in the fourth grade—maybe in the whole school! He'll probably win first prize."

"They give prizes?" I whispered to Jesse, but she didn't have a chance to answer. Miss Norton was already explaining.

"There will be an award given for the best piece of artwork in each grade," she explained. "Nobody here has to enter if he or she doesn't want to, of course. But I hope all of you will give this your best shot. You can work individually or in groups of any size you like."

Liza Toddley raised her hand and adjusted her thick glasses on her nose. "What kind of art do you want us to make?" she asked. Liza is a

teacher's pet. She's always trying to do things t
impress the teachers.

Miss Norton smiled. "It's not really about
what *I* want you to do. What's important is that
you let your own creativity be your guide," she
said. "The show's theme this year is 'Living
with Art,' so you can do just about anything you
like—painting, sketching, sculpture, whatever."

"'Living with Art'?" Rusty called out. "Oh
well, there goes my idea to sculpt something out
of stinky cheese."

Cole giggled and then held his nose. "There's
no way I'd want to live with *that*!"

Miss Norton smiled and shook her head.
Some teachers get annoyed when Rusty and
Cole clown around, but Miss Norton never
seems to get upset about anything.

"You all have one week to work on your
projects, so there's no time to waste," said Miss
Norton. "Go ahead and decide on your groups
while I set up the slide projector. I've brought
slides of some of the previous years' entries to

inspiration."

ssroom started buzzing as people
br... ...o groups. Nearby, I saw Cole and Rusty
trade a high five and guessed that they were
planning to work together.

"If we all work together, I know we can come
up with an amazing art project by next Friday,"
Maya said to us. "Lola's a really good artist, and
Amy's so creative with her scrapbooks, and Pia's
great at matching colors and stuff from being so

interested in fashion . . ."

Lola's eyes sparkled as she nodded. "This is so awesome," she exclaimed. "My mom was asked to judge the Annual Spring Art Show a couple of years ago. She got to help decide who won the prizes. The winners get their pictures in the newspaper and everything."

I glanced over at Cole and Rusty. "Should we ask the boys to be in our group, too?"

Lola wrinkled her nose. "No way," she said. "Cole is totally obsessed with comic books right now. I'm sure he'll want to sculpt Batman's boot or something."

Sure enough, Cole and Rusty came running over a second later. "Hey, we just decided we're going to make a poster with comic book art," Cole said. "Do you guys want to help?"

"Thanks, but no thanks." Jesse rolled her eyes. "But good luck with your idea."

"It's going to be so cool. We'll have to buy a bunch of new comic books as reference," Cole told Rusty.

❀ || ❀

Suddenly Rusty got a worried look on his face. It was that same look he had gotten during the talent show rehearsals when we talked about having to buy our costumes. Luckily Cole noticed Rusty's expression, too. Cole leaned over and whispered to Rusty, "Don't worry. I'll buy the comics with my allowance."

Rusty looked relieved and said, "Okay, but I'll pay you back when I get the money from my paper route."

Cole and Rusty grinned. "None of us should get our hopes up," Cole said. "Everybody knows Stanley always wins every prize that has anything to do with art."

"Yeah," Rusty added. "Even Lola can't compete with Mr. Superstar Artist."

I glanced over at Stanley. He was sitting by himself, already busy sketching something on a piece of paper. I guessed that meant he was planning to work on his own. Several other students also seemed to be going solo, while others were discussing their projects in groups of two or three. For instance, Liza had joined up with her friends Jennifer and Gracie. That was no surprise. The three of them did everything together—including acting snobby.

Cole and Rusty ran back to their own table. Lola glanced around at the rest of us.

"Okay, are we decided?" she said. "The five of us are going to work together to create the coolest art project Maple Heights has ever seen, right?"

"Yeah!" Jesse cheered.

"Whoo-hoo!" Maya added.

"Let's do it!" I cried.

I glanced over at Pia. She was staring into space again. Lola had noticed, too.

"Pia?" Lola reached over and touched Pia's shoulder. "Are you okay?"

"Huh?" Pia blinked. "Oh. Um, sure. I'm listening. Art project. Right."

Lola laughed. "Hey, don't fall over with excitement or anything," she joked.

Pia smiled weakly. "Look, I think the slide

show's starting," she said, pointing toward the front of the room.

We spent the rest of the class period looking at Miss Norton's slides and then paging through the art room's collection of books and magazines for inspiration. By the time we left for lunch, none of us had any brilliant project ideas yet. But I wasn't too worried. I was sure we would come up with something incredible.

During lunch, the five of us, plus Cole and Rusty, were sitting at our usual table in the cafeteria. We were all talking nonstop about the art show. Well, not quite *all* of us. Pia was hardly saying anything at all. I wasn't even sure she was listening.

Jesse noticed Pia's quiet mood, too. "What's wrong with you?" Jesse asked her. "You're acting weird. Don't you still want to be in our group?"

"Duh." Pia frowned. "Did I say that I didn't?"

Yikes! Pia sounded downright snippy. That *definitely* wasn't like her at all! What in the world was wrong with Pia?

Chapter 3

I shot a quick look at Jesse. She was scowling at Pia. Jesse isn't the most patient person in the world. I was afraid that she and Pia were going to have a real argument.

"It's okay, Pia," I said quickly. "This project is going to be a ton of fun, just wait! We'll probably come up with something so great we'll win the entire contest!"

"Dream on, Amy," Rusty joked. "We already told you—"

"Yeah, yeah, we know," Lola said as she flapped her hands at him as if shooing away a fly. "Stanley's going to win everything. That doesn't mean we're not going to give him a run for his money!"

"Yeah!" Maya added with a grin. "Our project will be great." She paused and bit her lip. "Um, if we ever come up with one, that is . . ."

"We will." Lola sounded confident. "We can brainstorm tomorrow at the tree house."

Jesse nodded. "Great idea. But we shouldn't waste any time between now and then, either. So let's all think about it tonight, okay? Then we can each bring our best idea to the tree house to get our brainstorming session going."

"That sounds like a good plan," Maya said.

"Definitely," I agreed. Jesse can be a little bossy, but sometimes her taking charge comes in handy. Her plan really did sound like a good one. With all of us thinking about it tonight, how could we *not* come up with the greatest project ever?

Even Pia nodded. "Wait," she said. "What was that about the tree house?"

Lola laughed. "I knew you weren't paying attention earlier," she teased playfully. Then she told her about the plan again.

"So you'll be there, right?" Jesse said.

"Sure." Pia shrugged. "Why not? My social calendar is totally open this weekend."

That sounded more like the regular Pia. Sort of, anyway. She still looked kind of grumpy.

But I tried not to worry about it. After all, we were Pia's best friends. If something was wrong, she would tell us.

I chewed on the end of my pencil and stared down at the sheet of paper on my desk. It was blank except for a ton of eraser marks and a few doodles of the nickname that my friend Lola had given me—Amy Hodgepodge. I'd been brainstorming ideas for the art project since I'd gone up to my room after dinner. But so far everything I thought of sounded lame.

"Coming up with a great idea is a lot harder than I expected," I murmured. I looked down at my dog, Giggles. Just seeing him sitting there by my feet made me feel a teensy bit better. Until he let out a superloud burp. "Pew-wee," I said holding my nose. "Smells like you've been eating rotten eggs, Giggles!"

I used the piece of paper I had been doodling

on as a fan to help clear the air. As I waved the
paper in front of my face, I caught sight of my
Amy Hodgepodge doodles. I smiled. Lola had
given me that nickname because I am Japanese,
Korean, African American, and White.

"Hodgepodge," I said aloud. "Hmm. Maybe
that's an idea, Giggles . . ."

I quickly wrote down the idea that had just

popped into my head: COLLAGE . . . MAYBE OF PHOTOS OF ALL OUR PETS?

"No," I said aloud, already flipping over the pencil to erase what I'd just written. "That won't work. Jesse and Maya don't have any pets."

I sighed again. This was definitely harder than it seemed! And I didn't have much more time. My bedtime was in half an hour, and then there would only be a short time in the morning before I had to meet my friends at the tree house. What if I couldn't come up with any good ideas before then?

"Maybe we could do a model of the tree house," I mumbled. I started to write the word *model* but quickly erased it again. A model of the tree house wasn't anywhere near original or interesting enough to enter in an art show.

Leaning down, I ruffled Giggles's short, wiry fur. He jumped to his feet and barked, wagging his stubby tail.

"It's weird, Giggles," I whispered, grabbing him and cuddling him on my lap. "Even though they're my best friends, I'm kind of nervous about this brainstorming meeting tomorrow. What if they think my ideas are stupid?"

Giggles started wriggling. He has too much energy to sit still for long. I let him jump down off my lap, then watched as he sniffed around on the floor.

Never mind, I told myself. *I was worried about what they'd think if I messed up at the talent show, too, and just look how well that turned out!*

That thought made me smile. When I first started at Emerson, my friends had invited me to enter the school talent show with them. I have a whole page about it in my scrapbook.

Thinking about my scrapbook gave me an idea. Maybe I could look in there for inspiration! I walked to my bookcase, pulled out my scrapbook, and carried it over to my bed.

Flopping down on my stomach, I paged through the scrapbook. The beginning was mostly pictures of my family and my old house, along with Giggles, of course. Then came the pages from after I'd started school at Emerson. There were pages for the talent show, my birthday party, the fourth grade's overnight camping trip, the Maple Heights Girls' Basketball League games I'd played in with my friends, and many more.

"That's it!" I cried so suddenly that Giggles let out an excited yip and started running around in circles.

"That's what?" my mom asked from the doorway. She smiled and came into the room.

I grinned at her. "I just had an idea for our art project, Mom," I told her. "And I'm pretty sure my friends are going to love it!"

Chapter 4

Jesse looked at her watch, then tapped her pen on her pad impatiently. "Pia's already like ten minutes late."

Jesse, Lola, Maya, and I were in the tree house. I'd brought over a batch of my grandmother's cookies, as promised, and we'd already eaten at least half of them. Since Pia hadn't arrived to help make the lemonade, Lola had brought out some juice boxes from her house.

"I know I told her the right time yesterday," Lola grumbled, leaning over to look out the tree house door to see if Pia was coming. "Do you think she forgot? She seemed kind of distracted yesterday."

"Maybe she's just being fashionably late," I joked. "Get it? *Fashionably* late?" Pia is a total fashion diva. She loves shopping and designing her own clothes and knows everything about all the latest styles.

"Very funny, Amy," Jesse grumbled. "I just wish Pia remembered to get here fashionably on time instead."

"I'm sure she'll be here soon." Maya sneaked a peek at her own watch, looking worried. "Let's just give her a few more minutes, okay? We should all be here before we start talking about our ideas."

My palms felt sweaty. Even though I still thought my idea was good, I was getting more nervous by the second at the thought of explaining it to the others. What if they didn't like it?

"Hey, I see someone coming." Lola leaned farther out the doorway and started waving. "Hey, Pia! Hurry and get up here already!"

A minute later Pia's face appeared at the top of the ladder. She climbed into the tree house and sat down without saying anything.

"What took you so long?" Jesse asked. "We've been waiting for you."

Pia shrugged. "I'm here now," she said. "So you don't have to wait anymore."

Jesse frowned. For a second I thought she was going to get mad. On the one hand, I could see why. Pia hadn't even apologized for showing up late. But that wasn't really worth fighting about, was it?

"Let's get started," Lola said. "Who wants to tell their idea first?"

Maya raised her hand. "I'll go," she said with

a giggle. "But I should warn you, my idea isn't very good."

"I'm sure it's great." Lola smiled at her. "Go ahead."

Maya shrugged. "Well, I was thinking about that slide Miss Norton showed us of the painting those kids did of their apartment building last year," she said. "We could do something like that—only we would do a painting of Emerson."

Jesse wrote it down. But she didn't look very impressed. "That would be okay, I guess," she said. "But like you said, those other kids just did sort of the same thing last year. We should try to come up with something more original."

"Yeah, Jesse's right," Lola said. "Sorry, Maya."

"It's okay," Maya said.

"I'll go next," Lola said. "My dad has some really huge sheets of poster board that he uses at work. I was thinking we could do a mural on one of them."

"Interesting." Jesse wrote it down. "What would the mural be about?"

Lola shrugged. "I don't know," she admitted. "I hadn't gotten that far yet."

"Hmm. Well, we'll have to think about it. Let's hear Amy's idea first," Jesse said.

"Do I have to go next?" I said quickly. I was even more nervous about sharing my idea since nobody seemed excited about Maya and Lola's suggestions. What if they didn't think mine was anything special, either?

"Okay, I'll go. We could do . . ." Jesse began, then let her voice trail off. She wants to be an actress or a singer or something like that, and so she's always practicing stuff like dramatic pauses. Finally she went on. ". . . a sculpture! It could be of a dancer—I could even pose for it if you want. I've seen lots of sculptures of dancers in museums—it would be totally artistic."

"I guess," Maya said slowly. "But can any of us sculpt well enough to pull off something like that?"

"No way." Lola shook her head. "Not in a week, anyway."

For a second Jesse looked insulted. But then she shrugged and smiled. "Yeah, maybe you're right," she said, crossing out what she'd just written on her pad.

"Okay, Pia. It's your turn," Maya said. "What's your idea?"

"Oh, I don't know." Pia shrugged. "Maybe we could do a model or something."

"A model of what?" Lola asked.

Pia shrugged again. "Anything you want," she said. "Our neighborhood, this tree house . . ."

The others didn't look very excited about that idea, either, though Jesse wrote it down with the others. I was glad I hadn't settled for the tree house model idea myself. Even so, I was still nervous. If none of my friends had managed to come up with any great ideas, what made me think mine was any better?

"You're up, Amy." Lola turned toward me. "And I hope your idea is brilliant, because right now all we've got is Cornball City!" She quickly glanced around at the others. "No offense, guys."

I noticed that my palms were sweating and that my heart was beating a little fast. Why was I being so silly? After all, these were my best friends. I took a deep breath. This was it!

"My idea—um, well, it was sort of inspired by my—um, my scrapbook," I began.

"You want us to do a scrapbook for the art show?" Jesse said, looking confused. "I don't know if that's really—"

"Hang on," Lola interrupted her. "Amy didn't say we should *do* a scrapbook, she said her idea was *inspired* by her scrapbook."

"Right," I said. "The theme of the contest is 'Living with Art,' right? Well, my idea is to do something called 'Living Art,' where all of us will actually be part of our project."

"Part of our project?" Maya leaned forward, looking curious. "What do you mean, Amy?"

Actually, she wasn't the only one who looked interested. Lola and Jesse did, too. Even Pia was focused on what I was saying.

"What we would do is trace ourselves onto a

big sheet of cardboard—or maybe one of those big poster boards Lola was talking about." I turned and smiled at her. "Then we'd cut out holes where our faces would be. We'd decorate the rest however we want—we could paint on our arms and legs, then maybe get some cool fabrics and funny wigs and stuff to decorate our clothes and bodies, and we could glue everything onto the picture. At the show, we'd stand it up and stick our faces through the holes. See? It would be sort of like we were in our own giant scrapbook page."

"I love it!" Lola clapped her hands. "It's sort of like those cutouts at amusement parks where you can stick your head through so it looks like you're a cowboy or something."

"Only better," Maya exclaimed. "Because we'll be looking like *us* in our own life-size scrapbook. We can even paint a border around it and then give it a caption like Amy does in her scrapbook—how about 'Five Best Friends'?"

Jesse was nodding as she scribbled notes on her pad. "Perfect. This whole idea is awesome," she said. "It'll be like 3-D, life-size art. The judges will love it!"

"Never mind that," Lola said. "The most important thing is that it'll be totally fun to make. I definitely want to go on the shopping trip to pick out the fabric and wigs and stuff!"

Maya giggled. "Okay," she said. "But maybe you should take Pia with you as a fashion consultant so we don't all end up looking like fashion disasters!"

That made me realize that Pia was the only one who hadn't said anything about my idea. I looked over at her. She was staring at the floor. I couldn't tell if she was even paying attention.

Jesse noticed, too. "Pia?" she said. "What do you think of Amy's idea? Pretty fantastic, huh?"

"Fantastic?" Pia finally looked up at the rest of us. "Um, not exactly. I actually think it sounds kind of dumb."

The smile froze on my face. For a second I couldn't even breathe. It felt as if Pia had punched me in the stomach or something instead of just insulting my idea.

"Are you kidding?" Lola exclaimed. "Did you even *hear* the idea? It's total genius!"

Maya nodded vigorously. "Amy's idea is really creative, Pia. Maybe if she explained it again . . ."

"No, I got it the first time. I just don't think it's that great, okay?" Pia snapped.

Jesse dropped her pen and paper and crossed her arms over her chest, staring at Pia. "What's your problem, anyway?" she demanded. "We all think Amy's idea is awesome. If you hate it so much, maybe you should just do something on your own."

"Fine." Pia jumped to her feet. "Maybe I will."

"Pia, wait . . ." Maya began soothingly.

But it was too late. A second later, Pia was gone.

Chapter 5

When I got home later that afternoon, I found my grandmother planting flowers in front of our house. She looked up when she heard me coming.

"Hello, Little Mitsukai," she greeted me.

That's her nickname for me. It means "Little Angel" in Japanese.

"Hi, Obaasan. Would you like some help?" I asked.

"I'd love some," she said. "And some company, too. Why don't you pull the weeds in that section so I can plant these petunias?"

"Okay." I went over and started pulling out the dandelions and other weeds that had popped up in the garden beds since the weather had turned warm. Normally I love helping Obaasan garden, especially in the spring. But today my heart wasn't really in it.

I was still thinking about what had
happened earlier. My friends and I had all been
surprised when Pia had stormed out of our
meeting. Lola had even climbed down to try to
get her to come back. But by the time she got
down the ladder, Pia was nowhere in sight.

The rest of us still had fun planning our
project, but it wasn't the same without Pia.
Plus, I couldn't stop thinking about the way
she'd insulted my idea. It would have been bad

enough if she'd said she didn't like it. But she hadn't—she'd said it was dumb.

"Is something wrong?" Obaasan asked. "Your eyes are a million miles away."

I blinked, realizing she was gazing at me. "Sorry, Obaasan," I said. "I guess I'm a little distracted."

Obaasan dug into the soft brown dirt with her small hand spade. "Would you like to talk about it?" she asked.

"I guess," I said. Maybe talking over what had happened would help me understand it better. I told Obaasan all about the art show and the meeting at the tree house and then about sharing my idea. "Lola and Jesse and Maya all thought it was great and wanted to do it," I finished.

My grandmother nodded. "I'm not surprised. It's a very good idea, Little Mitsukai."

"Thanks." I smiled at her. Then my smile faded as I remembered what came next. "The trouble was, Pia didn't like it at all. She said it was dumb."

"Well, sometimes when someone says something mean about someone else, it has less to do with the person being insulted than it does with the one doing the insulting," Obaasan said.

I tilted my head, trying to work that out in my head. "Wait," I said. "So you think Pia saying my idea is dumb isn't really about me at all? It's about Pia?"

"Something like that." Obaasan smiled at me, making the corners of her dark eyes crinkle. "You said Pia has not been herself lately, yes? Perhaps she is upset about something and is taking it out on you—her friends—because she doesn't know how to talk about it."

"I guess that makes sense," I agreed slowly. "She's not just acting snippy and weird with me. She's acting that way with all of us."

It made me feel a little bit better to know that Pia probably didn't hate me. But what she'd said about my project idea still hurt. And nothing my grandmother could say was likely to change that.

❀ ❀ ❀

"Here we are." My father pulled to the curb by the bus stop. It was Monday morning, and he'd offered to drop me off there on his way to work. Actually, he'd offered to drive me to school. But I liked riding the bus with my friends, so I'd asked him just to take me as far as the bus stop.

But when I looked out the window, I wished I'd let him take me all the way to school this time. That's because there was only one other person at the bus stop so far—Pia. I gulped, flashing back to her mean comment on Saturday.

I climbed out of the car and my father drove away. I walked as slowly as I could toward the corner, hoping that Lola and Cole or Maya or Jesse would arrive before I got there. As I walked, I kept my eyes on the sidewalk. But I could still feel Pia watching me.

"Hi," I muttered out of the corner of my mouth. I didn't want to be rude by not saying anything. But I also didn't want to give her a chance to insult me again. So I just kept staring at the ground.

I heard her clear her throat. "Um, Amy?" she said.

Her voice didn't sound snippy. Actually, she sounded kind of upset.

I sneaked a peek at her. She looked upset, too.

"I'm sorry, Amy!" she blurted out, taking a step toward me. "You look really bummed out, and I think I know why. I was so mean to you at the tree house this past weekend. I feel terrible about it, especially since your idea wasn't dumb at all—it was great!"

"Oh. Thanks." I was surprised, but relieved, too. "But then why did you say it was dumb in the first place?"

She shrugged and looked away. "I don't know. I guess I was just in a bad mood."

I remembered what my grandmother had said—that Pia might be acting weird because she was upset about something. If that was true, it was my job as her friend to try to help her. Wasn't it?

I took a deep breath and hoped I wasn't about to make her mad again. "It seems like you've been in a bad mood for a few days," I said. "Um, is anything wrong?"

Pia's face scrunched up and her cheeks turned red. At first I thought she was going to yell at me. Instead she started to cry.

"You can't tell anyone, Amy," she blurted out. "I don't want people to know! Do you promise not to tell?"

"I promise," I said, feeling confused. I put a hand on her shoulder. "Pia, what's the matter? You can tell me—I want to help."

She wiped her eyes with both hands. "Okay, you know how I went to visit my dad last week, right?"

I nodded. "You said he called and wanted to come pick you up and drive you out to his house for the afternoon."

"I thought it was because he got my e-mail about that big sale at the mall near his house." Pia sighed. "But it turned out he didn't even remember about that. He just wanted to tell me his big news in person—he and his new wife are going to have a baby."

I gasped. "Oh, wow!" I exclaimed. "You're

going to have a baby sister or brother? That's
so cool! But wait—why are you so upset? A new
baby is good news, right?"

Pia's eyes welled up with tears again. "You
don't get it," she cried. "Ever since my dad met
his new wife, I hardly see him. Once there's a
new baby, too—a whole new family—he probably
won't have any time for me at all!"

"Oh." Now I got it. "I see what you mean. But
I'm sure your dad will still make time for you.
He—"

"Shhh!" Pia's eyes widened. "Here comes Lola.
Remember, you promised not to tell anyone!"

"I know." I glanced over my shoulder at Lola,
wishing Pia would tell her about her father's new
baby, too. Lola always knows the right thing to
say. She might be able to make Pia feel better.
But I knew I couldn't breathe a word about
this—not without breaking my promise. "Don't
worry," I told Pia. "Your secret is safe with me."

Chapter 6

"How about this one?" Lola grabbed a spiky blond wig with purple highlights and pulled it onto her head.

I giggled. She looked pretty silly, especially since her own frizzy hair was still sticking out around the edges.

"It's totally you," I joked.

Then I glanced at the wall of wigs in front of us. There were tons of them. Some were normal shades of brown, black, blond, or red. Others, like the one Lola was wearing, were wild and silly. I looked over my shoulder at the rest of the store. It was crammed full of colorful fabrics and craft supplies.

"No wonder Jesse and Maya were so happy to let us volunteer to do all the shopping for our project," I said. "I don't know how we're ever going to decide what to get. There's so much stuff here to choose from!"

Right after school my mother had driven Lola and me over to Tisdale Street, the main shopping area in our part of the city. Now we were at Chapman's Craft Shack. My mom was in the back dropping off a picture she needed to have framed while Lola and I wandered around the rest of the store shopping for supplies for our project.

"Come on." Lola tossed the wig back on the rack. "Let's save the wigs for last. We should look at the fabrics again. I still can't decide whether Jesse would look better in the pink stuff you found or that cool orange material with the embroidery on it."

We wandered back over to some racks of fabric. I reached out to feel some hot pink silky stuff with little rhinestone dots all over it. "I still like this one, but I don't know if Jesse will," I said.

"I know," Lola agreed. "She hardly ever

wears pink. Maybe we should get it for Maya instead."

I bit my lip, trying to picture Maya wearing the fabric. "This is hard!" I exclaimed. "I wish Pia were here—she's the fashion expert. She'd probably know exactly what all of us should wear on our project."

"Yeah, maybe," Lola said with a frown. "But only if you could get her to pay attention long enough. I know Pia said that she still wants to be in our group, but I'm not so sure. She hasn't seemed that into it from the beginning. Plus, she was way rude to you on Saturday."

"It was no big deal," I said quickly. "Besides, she apologized for that."

"She did?" Lola looked surprised. "When? You didn't tell me that."

With a gulp, I wondered if I'd said too much. I was used to telling my friends everything. It wasn't easy keeping a secret from them— especially Lola.

"Um, at the bus stop this morning," I said

uncertainly. "It was right before you got there."

"Oh." Lola shrugged. "Well, anyway, it's probably better that she's not here. She's not exactly a barrel of laughs these days."

I didn't say anything as Lola went back to searching through the fabrics. If only she knew why Pia had been acting so different, I was sure she'd be a lot more understanding.

But I couldn't tell Lola, I reminded myself. I'd promised Pia I wouldn't.

I did my best to forget about Pia as we went back to our shopping. Soon we'd picked out a bunch of fabrics, along with some fun trimmings like rhinestones and ribbons and beads. We'd also found glue and paint and all the other stuff on our list. Chapman's seemed to have everything!

We were back at the wig wall when my mom found us. "How's it going, girls?" she asked.

"We're almost finished, Mom." I grabbed a straight, glossy black wig off the rack. "All we need to do is pick out the perfect hair."

Lola nodded as she pulled on a wig. "The rest of our stuff is over there if you want to see it, Mrs. Hodges," she said, pointing to the overflowing shopping cart we'd parked nearby.

My mom looked into the cart. "Wow, you guys found a lot of stuff!" she said. "I'll tell you what— I'll take this up front so Mrs. Chapman can start ringing it up. Just bring your wigs up when you're ready."

"Okay. Thanks, Mom. We won't be long." I pulled on the long brown wig. "What do you think? Could we trim this down to make it look like Pia's hair?"

Lola barely glanced at the wig. "I guess," she said. "But do you really think we should waste our money buying it? She'll probably just quit again."

"She won't do that," I said quickly, pulling off the wig.

"Well, don't tell anyone, but I sort of almost wish she would." Lola shrugged. "I know that's mean, and she's our friend and everything. But she's just been acting so weird lately!"

I felt terrible hearing her say that. "You
don't understand," I blurted out. "It's only
'cause she's upset about her dad!"

As soon as the words came out, I gasped and
clapped both hands over my mouth. But it was
already too late. Lola immediately dropped the

wig she was holding and turned toward me.

"What do you mean, Pia's upset about her dad?" she demanded.

Now I felt more terrible than ever. I'd promised Pia I wouldn't tell, but I hadn't even been able to keep the secret for one whole day. Still, maybe it was for the best. If Lola knew the real story, she might be able to help.

I took a deep breath and looked around the store to make sure nobody else would overhear me. "You have to promise not to tell anyone, okay?"

"I promise," Lola said. "Now spill it, Amy!"

"Pia's dad and his new wife are having a baby," I said. "He told her when she went to visit him last week."

"I'm confused. Isn't a new baby a good thing?" asked Lola.

I shrugged. "She thinks with a new baby around, her dad might forget about her."

Lola nodded, rubbing her chin thoughtfully. "Yeah, I guess she doesn't even see him that much now, so I can't blame her for being worried. This totally explains her funky mood lately. We should be extra nice to her from now on."

"Definitely," I said. "But don't forget—it's a secret. I wasn't supposed to tell anyone, so you can't, either."

"Don't worry about me." Lola stuck out her hand and we pinkie-swore. "I won't tell a soul."

Chapter 7

"There." Maya finished gluing down a piece of denim fabric that she'd cut out to look like a pair of jeans. "How does that look?"

I stood up to see. Lola's dad had dropped off a huge piece of poster board at school that morning. It was too big to fit on any of the art room tables, so Miss Norton had helped us clear a spot in the corner so we could work on the floor. We'd spent the first part of art period tracing our outlines onto the poster board. Now Lola was carefully cutting out our faces with a craft knife while the rest of us started decorating the poster board. Everyone loved the supplies we'd bought at Chapman's. Jesse, Pia, and I were each working on the clothes for our own figures.

"Wow, that looks perfect, Maya," I said. "It

makes it look like you're wearing real jeans!"

Lola glanced over, too. "Yeah, it looks great," she said. "If you want to decorate the jeans to make them look even more exciting, we have plenty of rhinestones."

"Rhinestones?" asked Pia. "That's so last century."

"Well, we like them," said Lola. "Go ahead and glue them on, Maya."

Maya's eyes widened. "Oh, I don't know," she said. "I'm afraid I might mess it up. Can one of you guys do it?"

"I will," Jesse volunteered, glancing up from where she was cutting out some purple fabric with a pair of scissors. "Just give me a second to finish this."

"Okay, thanks." Maya sounded relieved. "Maybe I'll start painting in all of our arms and legs. All I have to do to make that look good is stay inside the lines!"

"Good point!" I agreed with a laugh.

Then I stood up and stretched. I'd been

crouched over the poster board for so long that my shoulders were getting cramped.

Glancing around the room, I could see that everyone else was hard at work, too. Cole and Rusty were at a small table near our corner. The boys had another piece of poster board from Cole and Lola's dad's office, though theirs was a little smaller than ours. I stepped closer to take a look and saw that they were using a ruler to draw a series of boxes like a comic book panel.

At the next table, Jennifer, Liza, and Gracie were crafting a bunch of colorful papier-mâché flowers. Nearby, Yasmin and Evelyn were making something out of Popsicle sticks and pom-poms. And up at the front of the room, Stanley Hermann was working on molding a clay sculpture. It looked sort of like a human head.

Miss Norton was wandering around the room offering advice to everyone. She stopped in front of Stanley's sculpture.

"Wonderful work, Stanley!" she exclaimed loudly enough for the whole room to hear. "Very lifelike. I already knew you were an extraordinarily gifted artist, but I'm impressed anew!"

I heard a snort from nearby. Glancing over, I saw Cole and Rusty rolling their eyes at each other and making goofy faces. I realized they were making fun of Stanley because of what the teacher had said, and I frowned.

The boys are probably jealous because they think Stanley is going to win first prize, I thought, turning back to glance down at our project. *But I'm not so sure he will. Our "Living with Art" scrapbook page is going to be awesome!*

My shoulders were all stretched out, so I crouched down again and went back to work. I was so focused on what I was doing that I hardly noticed when Jesse and Pia started to argue.

"No way!" Jesse was complaining when I finally looked up to see what was happening.

"Maya already said I could do it!"

"That's because Maya is even more fashion-challenged than you are." Pia folded her arms across her chest. "If we want this to look halfway decent, you've got to let me do it!"

"I thought you didn't like rhinestones, Pia," said Jesse.

"I don't, but if you're going to do it anyway . . ." said Pia.

Maya looked worried. "It's okay, you guys," she said. "I'm sure the rhinestones will look great no matter who glues them on."

I realized they were arguing about who got to glue the rhinestones onto Maya's jeans on the poster board. It sounded like Pia thought she was the best one for the job, even though it was already settled that Jesse was going to do it.

Pia grabbed the bottle of glue off the floor. "Grow up, Jesse," she said. "I'm gluing the rhinestones, and that's that."

"No! Maya said I could do it." Jesse snatched the glue out of her hands.

"Hey!" Pia looked outraged. She dove toward Jesse, trying to grab the glue back. The two of them ended up in a tug-of-war.

"Stop it, you two!" Maya cried, reaching for the glue.

But she was too late. Jesse and Pia were squeezing the bottle too hard, and glue came squirting out. Jesse jumped back just in time, but the glue ended up all over Pia and Maya!

"Ew!" Maya cried. "It's all over me!"

"Me too." Pia stared down at her shirt in horror. "And this is a brand-new top! Come on, we'd better get permission to go to the bathroom and wash this off before it dries."

Pia glared at Jesse one last time, then she and Maya hurried off toward Miss Norton.

"What's with Pia, anyway?" she complained. "She's being such a pain! It's like some aliens came and replaced her personality with Jennifer's!"

Lola and I exchanged a glance. I could tell she was thinking the same thing I was. If Jesse knew why Pia was in such a bad mood, she wouldn't say something like that.

"You know Pia," Lola said quickly. "She feels really strongly about fashion. She probably thought you might accidentally glue the rhinestones on in last season's pattern or something."

I forced a laugh. "Yeah," I said. "That's probably it."

But Jesse didn't even crack a smile. "Well, whatever it is, her bad mood is getting really old." She pointed to the figures on the poster board. "Good thing she's standing at one end of our picture. If she doesn't shape up, we should tell her we're going to cut her out of our project!"

"Don't be like that, Jesse," Lola said quickly. "Poor Pia's been through enough lately."

"What do you mean?" Jesse asked with wide eyes.

I couldn't believe Lola would let something like that slip. It was one thing for me to mess up, but Lola was usually cool under pressure!

She shot me an anxious look. I was hoping she would try to talk her way out of it somehow.

But instead, Lola turned back to face Jesse. "Listen, you can't tell a soul," she whispered. "But I know why Pia's so upset—she just found out her dad's new wife is having a baby!"

Chapter 8

I was so shocked that I hardly heard a word as Lola explained the rest. I couldn't believe she'd spilled Pia's secret!

"You said you wouldn't tell!" I blurted out. "You pinkie-swore and everything!"

"Sorry," Lola replied, looking at the floor. "But it's only Jesse. After what just happened, I figured she deserved to know the scoop." She glanced at Jesse. "But you can't tell anyone else, not even Maya or the boys. You, me, and Amy are the only ones who know, and Pia doesn't even know I know."

"Don't worry, I won't say anything." Jesse didn't look mad anymore. "Poor Pia! I mean, I wasn't even that happy when I found out my mom was pregnant with my little sister, Maria. And she and my dad are still married and living in the same apartment and everything! Something like this would be way worse."

"Quiet," I hissed as the classroom door opened. "They're coming back."

"The glue rinsed right out," Maya announced cheerfully as she and Pia reached us. "Once our shirts dry, you probably won't be able to see what happened at all."

"Good." Jesse turned toward Pia with a huge, friendly smile. "I'm really sorry your new shirt almost got messed up, Pia. To make up for it, you can glue on the rhinestones if you want."

Pia looked surprised but pleased. "Okay, thanks," she said. "Maybe you could help me figure out where to put them?"

"No, that's okay." Jesse's smile was bigger than ever. "You'll do a much better job, Pia!"

I winced. Jesse sounded almost as sweet and cheerful and generous as Maya. Hearing her act like that was almost as weird as it would be if Maya suddenly started bossing everyone around.

Luckily, Pia didn't seem to notice a thing. She just grabbed the half-empty bottle of glue and a handful of rhinestones and went to work.

"Amy," my grandfather said as he stuck his head into my room. "It's almost dinnertime. Do you want to come and help your grandmother and me set the table?"

"Sure, Harabujy," I said. That was what I called him. He's Korean, and "Harabujy" is Korean for "grandfather."

I set down my English textbook. It wasn't as if I was getting much homework done, anyway. I was way too distracted by what had happened in art class to think about adverbs and prepositions. I still couldn't believe Lola had told Jesse Pia's secret!

"How was school today, Amy?" my grandmother asked as the three of us set the table. "Did you straighten things out with your friend Pia?"

"Sort of." I smoothed out a place mat. "I

mean, not exactly. Pia finally told me the reason she's been in such a bad mood." I almost blurted out the secret, but I stopped myself just in time. I'd learned my lesson! "I can't say what it is, though, because I promised her I wouldn't tell anybody."

"Good girl, Amy." My grandfather glanced up from setting out some silverware and nodded. "A secret told is a trust lost." I looked down at my feet and thought about what he had said for a moment.

After we'd finished setting the table, the three of us went into the living room and sat down on the couch. "But that's the trouble," I explained. "I sort of already told someone else. It was kind of an accident, though. And Pia doesn't know about it."

My grandparents exchanged a look. "I see," Obaasan said. "Well, I'm sure you didn't mean to break your promise. But all you can do now is own up to what you did. You should probably think about apologizing to your friend."

I gulped. "You mean you think I should tell Pia?" I said. "Um . . ."

On the one hand, I knew she was right. I'd made a choice to tell that secret, and now I might have to face the consequences—like my parents and grandparents had always taught me.

But in this case, was telling Pia really the best thing to do? She was already upset about her dad. If she knew I'd spilled her secret, it would only upset her more.

Besides, she was sure to tell Lola and Jesse and everyone else the whole story sooner or later. All we had to do was keep quiet until then, and after that everything would be fine.

"I'm glad we're having that extra art class instead of gym this afternoon," Lola said, taking a bite of her sandwich. It was lunch period on Wednesday. Cole and Rusty weren't sitting with us because they had a baseball team meeting. The rest of us were all talking about our art project.

Jesse nodded. "We should be able to get all the wigs glued on the poster board today."

"Right," I agreed. "Then all we'll have to do in class tomorrow is the caption. We can take our time and make sure the lettering looks really good."

Maya nodded and clapped her hands. "This is so exciting!" she exclaimed. "I can't believe our project is almost finished."

"Yeah." Jesse reached for her milk. "We're

going to win first prize for sure!"

"Whoo-hoo!" Lola cheered.

Pia laughed. She'd seemed slightly more cheerful yesterday and today. That made me glad I'd decided to go against my grandparents' advice and *not* tell her what I'd done.

"This is going to be really cool," she agreed.

Just then Jennifer, Liza, and Gracie strolled over to our table. "What's going to be cool, Pia?" Jennifer asked. She tossed her long, blond hair over one shoulder. "You aren't talking about your new baby sister or brother, are you? Because I know if it was *my* father who was having a kid with his new wife, I'd be totally bummed."

"Yeah," Liza added. "He probably won't have any time for you anymore with a cute new baby in his life."

Gracie giggled. "It's a good thing you have such great friends." She smirked at the rest of us. "They'll have to be like your family, since your dad has a new family now."

All three of them laughed snottily at that. Then

they turned on their heels and walked away.

I just sat there, feeling frozen in place. Lola and Jesse looked shocked, too. Maya looked confused. Pia just sat there, her face turning redder and redder with her fists balled up tight.

Then she whirled to face me. "How could you, Amy?" she yelled. "I trusted you! But obviously that was a mistake!"

Then she burst into tears. Leaping up from her seat, she raced out of the lunchroom before the rest of us could say a word.

Chapter 9

"I told you not to tell anyone!" I cried, glaring at Lola.

Lola spun around to face Jesse. "You are such a blabbermouth," she snapped at Jesse. "I should've known better than to trust you with a secret!"

"What are you yelling at me for?" Jesse protested. "I would never tell Jennifer or her friends anything! I didn't say a word to them, I swear. The only ones I told were Evelyn and Yasmin." She paused. "Oh yeah, and I guess Danny and Stanley might have overheard me talking about it, too, and maybe Angela . . ."

"Hang on a second." Maya held up both hands, looking perplexed. "What's going on here? Why is Pia so upset? What are you guys talking about?"

I sighed, figuring there was no point keeping
her in the dark. If Jennifer and her friends
knew, the whole school probably knew.

"Pia's dad is having a baby with his new
wife," I explained. "Pia told me at the bus stop
on Monday, and I accidentally told Lola."

"And I accidentally told Jesse," Lola put in.

I frowned at her. "It wasn't an accident,
Lola. You told her on purpose!"

"So you guys all knew except me?" Maya
sounded kind of upset. I guess she felt left
out. But I didn't have time to worry about

that. I was too furious with Lola and Jesse—but especially Lola. She'd been my very first friend at Emerson, and I'd thought I could trust her . . . no matter what.

"I wish I could've told you, Maya," Jesse said.

Lola rolled her eyes. "Why didn't you? You told the entire rest of the school, anyway."

"I did not!" Jesse narrowed her eyes. "Anyway, it's not like you're so great at keeping secrets, either. You told me, remember? And Amy started it when she told you. So we're all to blame!"

"Whatever!" Lola put up one hand with her palm toward Jesse.

"Don't 'whatever' me!" Jesse exclaimed. "I'm just telling the truth!"

"That's funny," Lola said. "Because whenever you open your big mouth, all I hear is blah blah blah!"

Jesse shoved back her chair and stood up, her eyes blazing. "Fine," she snapped. "Then maybe I won't talk to you anymore at all."

"Perfect!" Lola cried, jumping to her feet.

"While you're at it, neither of you should talk to me anymore, either," I blurted out, feeling so angry and betrayed that I could hardly think straight.

"Guys . . ." Maya began uncertainly.

But it was too late to try making peace this time. All three of us were already storming away from the table in different directions.

That afternoon during our extra art class, the five of us worked on our project in silence. Pia's eyes were red from crying, and she didn't look at anyone. Jesse scowled anytime one of us met her gaze. And Lola just kept whistling some annoying tune and acting like she didn't care. The only one who didn't look mad was Maya. She just looked worried. But she didn't say anything to the rest of us, either.

Finally I couldn't take it anymore. I had to get away for a minute. Setting down the glue I was using to attach my wig to the poster board, I headed toward the boys' table.

But Cole and Rusty weren't there. I spotted them whispering together near Stanley's table. Stanley was working so hard on his sculpture that he didn't notice them. His clay head was almost finished. It looked great. He'd sculpted hair on it and everything. If it hadn't been all clay colored, you might have thought it was a real head.

"Stanley's sculpture is really good, isn't it?" I said to Cole and Rusty.

Both boys jumped. I guess I'd surprised them.

"Yeah," Rusty said with a grin. "It's super-awesome. But I bet it could be even better with a little more, you know, creativity."

"Yeah," Cole agreed. "Miss Norton's always talking about being creative and thinking 'outside the box.' I bet she'd love Stanley's sculpture even more if it was more, um, creative!"

He and Rusty both started laughing. I rolled my eyes. I wasn't in the mood for their silliness. So I said good-bye and wandered slowly back toward my own work area—also known as the war zone.

❀ ❀ ❀

When I climbed on the bus that afternoon, I looked for Pia. She was sitting by herself near the middle of the bus. Lola was sitting beside Cole in the first seat, and Jesse was way in the back, two rows behind Maya.

Pia still looked pretty angry. I felt awful that she was so upset again just when it seemed like she was starting to feel better.

And the worst part was, she was so mad at me that there was nothing I could do to help her. She wouldn't even talk to me. Then again, I totally deserved it. I never should have told Lola that secret!

I saw Lola looking at me. I quickly avoided her gaze and walked down the aisle toward Pia's seat.

"Listen, Pia," I said tentatively, perching on the edge of the seat. "Can I talk to you for a second? I want to apologize. I never meant to—"

"Excuse me," Pia said icily, pushing me aside so she could stand up. "I think I'll go sit over there."

She marched down the bus aisle and plopped down beside Rory Fuwicki. He looked surprised. No wonder! Nobody likes to sit with Rory on the bus because he's always playing pranks on people. If Pia was distracted enough to sit down with him, she had to be even angrier than I'd thought. I slumped back against the seat, feeling hopeless.

"Hey," Lola said from right beside me.

I looked up. She was standing in the aisle right by my seat. I could tell she wanted me to scoot over so she could sit down, but I didn't. So she sat down behind me instead.

"I just wanted to say I'm really sorry, Amy," she said, leaning over the seat. "I guess I shouldn't have told Jesse about Pia, but . . ."

I didn't want to hear any more. So I stuck my

fingers in my ears and stared straight ahead. After a few seconds she shrugged and went back to sit with Cole.

Taking my fingers out of my ears, I stared at the back of the seat in front of me. *Oh well*, I thought. *It was nice having friends for a while.*

I was thinking of asking my parents if I could go back to homeschooling when Cole came back to my seat. "Hey," he said. "Guess what? Jesse just came up to Lola and tried to apologize."

"Oh, really?" I said. "Um, I mean, why should I care what they do?"

Cole rolled his eyes. "Move over," he said, shoving his way onto my seat. "Look, I'm just telling you because Lola closed her eyes and started humming so she wouldn't have to listen to her. That's why I'm here—I had to get away from that noise!"

Normally I would have laughed. But I wasn't in the mood for Cole's goofiness just then.

The bus driver climbed aboard and started the engine. Soon we were pulling out onto the street in front of the school.

I glanced over at Cole, feeling guilty for snapping at him. After all, it wasn't his fault his twin sister couldn't keep a secret.

"Did you guys get a lot done on your art project today?" I asked him. "It looked like you were almost finished when I saw it earlier."

"We'd better be, right?" Cole said. "The art show is the day after tomorrow!" He shot me a curious look. "I hope you girls are speaking to one another again by then."

I frowned and turned to stare out the window. Talking to Cole was fine, but not if all he wanted to talk about was my so-called friends! For the rest of the ride, every time he mentioned them, I just stared out the window again. In between he talked about other stuff and I tried to listen, but I was so furious and upset and worried that I hardly heard a word.

It was the worst bus ride of my life!

Chapter 10

That evening at dinner I didn't have much
of an appetite. I just pushed my food around on
the plate, thinking back over my terrible day. It
wasn't long before my family noticed.

"What's wrong, Amy?" my mom asked. "You're
awfully quiet."

"Nothing," I muttered.

All four of them exchanged a look. "Please,
Little Mitsukai," my grandmother said. "You
know you can talk to us. You're not still having
problems with your friends, are you?"

"Sort of." I felt confused and embarrassed
about everything that had happened. But maybe
I would feel better if I talked about it with my
family. So I caught my parents and grandparents
up on what had happened.

"I see," my dad said when I was finished.

"Well, I guess you must already realize it was wrong for you to break your promise and gossip, right?"

I nodded sadly. "I know," I whispered. "I really messed up this time. Pia's never going to forgive me!"

"I'm sure that's not true," my grandfather said. "She's your friend."

"Not anymore." I shook my head as I remembered the icy look she'd given me on the bus. "I told you, she just got up and sat somewhere else when I tried to apologize. I even tried again when we got off the bus, but she wouldn't even look at me!"

"Well, no wonder," my mother said. "You can't expect forgiveness from Pia when you won't forgive Lola."

I blinked. "Oh," I said. "I guess I never thought of it that way."

"Well, think about it." My dad reached for the pepper. "If you're a true friend, you forgive your friends even when they mess up."

"Your father speaks the truth, Amy." My grandfather raised one finger. "You cannot control whether someone else will forgive you or not. But you *can* control yourself—and choose to forgive your friends no matter how they've hurt you."

I nodded slowly. "Yeah," I said. "Maybe you're right . . ."

The next morning I was a little late to the bus stop. Everyone else was already there, including Lola. She saw me coming and stared at me anxiously.

I looked right back at her. Then I smiled and lifted my hand to wave hello. "Whew," I called to her. "Glad I made it. I was afraid I might miss the bus!"

Lola hurried over. "Amy, you have to listen to me this time," she exclaimed. "I'm really, really sorry. I didn't mean to break my word to you."

"I know. I forgive you. I'm sorry I wouldn't listen yesterday, but I guess I was still too mad. But it's not worth staying mad over something like this. I want to be friends again."

"Awesome!" Lola grinned, looking relieved.

I glanced over at Jesse. "Isn't there someone you want to forgive, too?"

"What do you mean?" Lola looked over at Jesse, too. At first she frowned, but after I told her about what my mother had said about forgiveness, she took a deep breath and thought for a moment. Then she said, "You're right. I'll be right back, Amy."

She ran over and let Jesse apologize. Then she forgave her. Soon all three of us were hugging. Maya hugged us all, too. It felt good that we were all talking again.

Just then we heard the rumble of the bus pulling around the corner. We climbed aboard

and found two seats together. I sat down with Lola, and Jesse sat with Maya.

"I wish Pia were here so we could try to apologize to her again," Lola said with a sigh. "But she has a dentist appointment this morning."

I'd forgotten about that. I wished we didn't have to wait to make things right with Pia. But now that the rest of us were speaking again, I felt more optimistic that everything would be okay soon.

"Never mind," I said. "That just gives us more time to come up with the best apology ever!"

❀ ❀ ❀

Pia didn't get to school until the very end of art class. While she was at the dentist we finished our project, including her part. We also talked about what to say to Pia to get her to forgive us. And we agreed that if she wouldn't, we would withdraw our project from the art show—after all, it was called "Five Best Friends," and we couldn't put it on display if only four of us were on speaking terms.

When she finally came into art class, Pia didn't look at any of us. I could tell right away that she was still upset. I traded a glance with Lola. Maybe this would be harder than I'd thought.

As soon as Miss Norton excused us to go to lunch, Pia jumped up and raced for the door. I was about to run after her, but Lola held me back.

"Just let her go," she said. "That way we can all apologize to her together in the cafeteria."

When we entered the lunchroom, Maya and Jesse were waiting for us. "Where's Pia?" Jesse asked.

"She should be here already." Lola looked across the room. "I don't see her at our table. Maybe she's in line."

But by the time the four of us went through the lunch line, Pia still wasn't at our table. "There she is!" Maya said, pointing.

I looked over and saw Pia sitting by herself at a table in the corner near the bathrooms.

Usually nobody sat way over there.

We walked over carrying our food. "Hey, Pia," Lola called. "What are you doing over here? Let's go to our table—we need to talk to you."

Pia didn't answer. She looked up at us for a second with a frown. Then she got up and ran into the girls' bathroom.

"Come on!" Jesse said, following her.

The rest of us ran after her. We got into the bathroom just in time to see Pia rush into a stall and lock the door.

"Pia!" Jesse cried. "Seriously, we know we were wrong. Come out so we can apologize!"

"Please, Pia?" Maya added in a soft voice.

But there was no answer. The only sound that came out of the stall was an occasional sniffle.

"Pia?" I took a step closer to the stall door. "This is all my fault. I never should have shared your secret, even with Lola."

"It's all our faults," Lola added. "We just wanted to help. But we ended up hurting you instead. We're really, really sorry."

Pia still didn't say a word. The four of us
exchanged a worried look. What now?

"Um, we're sorry about your dad, too, Pia,"
Lola said after a second. "But I'm sure things will
turn out okay."

"Right," Maya added. "It's fun being a big
sister."

"Yeah," Jesse agreed. She paused. "Well,
sometimes, anyway. It's definitely fun bossing my

little brother and sister around."

Lola laughed. "See, Pia? Maybe it won't be so bad."

"There's no way your dad will forget about you," I added.

"Amy's right," Lola agreed. "You'll always have a special place in his heart because you were his first kid."

We waited again. No response. I felt frustrated. How could we get Pia to forgive us if she wouldn't even come out?

I thought about what my grandfather had said last night. We couldn't force Pia to forgive us. If she wanted to stay mad and not be friends anymore, that was her choice. Meanwhile, I realized we had a choice to make, too.

"Listen, Pia," I said. "The art show is tomorrow morning. Our project is ready—we finished the caption in art class this morning without you. But we're not going to enter it without you."

"That's right, Pia." Maya spoke up. "Our

project is called 'Five Best Friends.' It wouldn't be right to do it without you."

"So if you don't want to forgive us, that's your decision," I continued. "We'll tell Miss Norton we want to withdraw our project from the show."

I held my breath, hoping that would make Pia say something or come out. But there was still no sound from inside the stall.

"Come on." Lola put a hand on my arm. "We should go finish our lunch."

With a sigh, I followed the others out into the cafeteria. We all sat down and tried to eat. I kept at least one eye on the bathroom door at all times, but Pia didn't come out for the rest of the lunch period.

Chapter 11

The next morning my mom drove me to school. My grandparents rode along, too. All family members were invited to come and see the art show. My dad had to work, but he promised to try to stop by later. All the projects would be on display for the whole weekend.

Well, all except ours, I thought sadly. I hadn't had the heart to tell my family that we might be withdrawing from the show. They would find out soon enough. Pia hadn't spoken to any of us all yesterday afternoon or on the bus on the way home, either. Jesse had wanted to march up to her and force her to listen to us, but Maya had talked her out of it.

"It's up to Pia now," she'd pointed out. "We can't make her be our friend again."

When we got to school, there was a huge

crowd of parents and other family members in the lobby. There were some tables set up there with coffee and pastries.

"I guess you guys should stay here," I told my family. "Principal Brewster will tell you when to go into the gym."

"All right," my mom said. "We'll see you in a few minutes, Amy."

Obaasan patted my arm. "I can't wait to see your creation, Little Mitsukai!"

I smiled weakly, then hurried down the hall to the gym. It was a madhouse inside. Students from every grade were milling around nervously. All the art projects were already set up along one wall. Each project had a cloth draped over it. Miss Norton had already explained that when the parents came in, the students would take turns unveiling their creations.

Lola, Jesse, and Maya were standing by our project. It looked enormous beneath its cloth. It was definitely the largest piece in the show.

"Is Pia here?" I asked them.

Lola shook her head sadly. "No sign of her."

I let out my breath with a whoosh. "Oh well. I guess we should go find Miss Norton and tell her we're withdrawing."

Before we could move, the gym doors flew open. Family members started pouring in, talking and laughing.

"This way, everyone!" Principal Brewster called out in his booming voice. "Find a spot with a good view, and we'll get started with the unveiling!"

"Uh-oh," Jesse said. "We should have withdrawn earlier."

"It's okay." Lola pointed. "It looks like they're starting at that end with Stanley's project. We should have plenty of time to tell Miss Norton before they get to us."

We started making our way down the line of projects toward the teacher. It wasn't easy since the gym was so crowded. By the time we were almost there, Stanley was getting ready to yank the covering off his sculpture. I paused, wanting to see how it had turned out.

I gasped when Stanley pulled back the cloth. Someone had stuck huge elephant ears and a big, goofy nose onto his sculpture!

Stanley looked horrified. "Hey!" he began.

But I could hardly hear him. The audience was applauding loudly. Miss Norton clasped her hands together, looking thrilled.

Just then I noticed Cole and Rusty. They

were standing nearby behind their own project. Both of them were practically doubled over with laughter.

"Oh, Stanley!" Miss Norton cried happily. "What a surprise! You must have worked awfully hard to finish this up without letting any of us see your final vision."

A stout man in a tweed suit stepped forward to peer at the sculpture. "It's really quite extraordinary," he said, jotting a note on the pad he was holding. "Rather reminiscent of the work of Salvador Dalí and other surrealists."

"That's the art critic from the newspaper," Lola whispered to me. "I think he likes it!"

A young woman with a fancy-looking camera on a tripod started taking photos of Stanley's sculpture.

Suddenly, I remembered what Rusty and Cole had said in class the other day. "I'll be right back," I told my friends. Then I hurried over to the boys. By the time I got there, they'd stopped laughing. They were listening as Miss Norton and the art critic kept gushing over Stanley's work.

"Did you do that?" I asked, pointing toward the sculpture. "Were you the ones who sabotaged Stanley's work?"

"We thought we did, but everyone loves it!" Cole said unhappily.

Rusty kicked at the base of the easel holding their poster. "Yeah. What a waste of time! Hey, maybe we should go take credit."

"No way, then we'd get busted," said Cole.

I frowned. I couldn't believe they'd done something so mean. Before I could say anything to the boys, Jesse ran over and dragged me away.

"Come on," she said. "We need to grab Miss Norton soon, before she gets to our project!"

But the teacher was already helping Jennifer and her friends unveil their paper flower display. Then she moved down the line to the boys' comic strip art and then to the next couple of projects. It was almost our turn.

"We've got to tell her—now," Lola whispered. "Pia still isn't here, and our project won't work without her."

I nodded. I just hoped my family wouldn't be too disappointed.

As I looked for Miss Norton, I noticed someone rushing into the gym. I gasped when I saw who it was.

"Pia!" I exclaimed. And her father was right behind her.

She spotted us and raced over, leaving her dad behind with the other parents. "I'm here, I'm here!" she cried breathlessly, skidding to a stop in front of us. "Oh my gosh, the traffic was so terrible I thought we'd never make it! Did I miss our big unveiling?"

Chapter 12

For a second I was so shocked that I couldn't say a word. So were my other friends. Meanwhile, Pia was looking over at our covered project.

"Oh, good!" she exclaimed. "I didn't miss it." Then she turned to face us and laughed. "Listen, I totally forgive you guys!"

"Really?" I blurted out. "Even me?"

"Especially you, Amy Hodgepodge." Pia grabbed me and hugged me. "I'm sorry I freaked out before. And I'm sorry I've been so grumpy lately. It's just, you know, my dad . . ."

"Yeah," Lola said. "We *all* know. That's sort of the problem, remember?"

That made everybody laugh. Soon we were all hugging one another. I was so relieved that I didn't know whether to laugh or cry.

"Check it out," Maya said. "They're coming!"

We all looked and saw the crowd, including Miss Norton and the art critic, moving toward our project. I grinned from ear to ear and waved at my mom and grandparents.

"Come on, Amy." Jesse yanked me under the cloth. "We have to get in position!"

We all huddled behind the poster board. "Wait, am I supposed to be here or here?" Maya whispered, hovering between two of the face holes. It was hard to remember the order from the back, where we couldn't see our bodies! I was glad my spot was right in the middle so I didn't have to worry.

"You're that one," Jesse hissed, pushing Maya to the correct spot. I got in place and stuck my head through the opening. It felt weird doing it with the cloth over our faces, especially since it smelled like dust.

Luckily, we didn't have long to wait. Miss Norton announced our names. "And here's their project," she went on. "They call it 'Five Best Friends'!"

Then she whipped off the cloth. I smiled and looked out at the audience. They all started to clap and cheer.

"Look! It's like a giant photo album!" someone cried.

"No, not a photo album," someone else said. "More like a scrapbook!"

I grinned. They got it!

The art critic gazed at us with a smile. "Well, now," he said. "I must say, this is one of the most creative ideas I've seen in a long time!"

"For real?" Jesse said from her spot at the far end.

For some reason that made the onlookers laugh, including the critic. I guess it looked pretty funny seeing a scrapbook page talk!

"For real," the critic replied. Then he turned to the photographer with the tripod. "Make sure you get a good shot of this one," he instructed her. "It's going on the front page of the art section this weekend for sure."

FIVE BEST FRIENDS

❃ ❃ ❃

After the rest of the projects were unveiled, Miss Norton asked everyone to stay with their projects for a while longer so everyone could walk around and take a closer look. So the five of us stayed where we were with our heads stuck through their holes. One of the first people to come by to see us was Pia's dad.

"You girls did a great job," he said, peering at the details of our project. "And I can definitely tell my daughter had a hand in it— your outfits are fabulous!"

Pia giggled. "Thanks, Daddy. We all worked really hard on it."

Her father reached out to touch her on the chin. "I'm proud of you, sweetheart."

Soon he moved on to look at some of the other projects. "Wow," Jesse said as soon as he was gone. "I guess things must be a little better between you two, huh?"

"Yeah," Pia replied happily. "I called him last night to talk about how I felt about the whole new baby thing. It felt good to finally talk about it and not just be impatient and crabby with you guys."

"So did you work things out?" Lola asked.

"Pretty much," Pia said. "He promised me that the new baby won't make him forget me. In fact, he said he'll probably need me to help out once the baby comes, so I'll probably be spending a lot more time at his house. After all, the baby will need a big sister to teach him or her all kinds of stuff. He even asked me to come up with a list of names for the baby."

"That's awesome!" I said. "See? I knew your dad wouldn't forget you."

Pia tilted her head so she could look over at me. "Thanks, Amy. And I'm sorry I got so mad at you."

"No, I'm sorry for breaking my promise to you." Even though I'd already said that, I figured it wouldn't hurt to say it one more time. "I never should have told anyone your secret. It just slipped."

"Well, I probably shouldn't have kept that big of a secret from my best friends in the first place," Pia replied. "Especially since it almost ruined our friendship."

"Never," Lola spoke up. "Nothing could ruin

things for Five Best Friends like us!"

❀ ❀ ❀

By the time Principal Brewster had awarded the prize ribbons—we tied with Stanley Hermann for first place in our grade—and all the parents had left, it was almost lunchtime. The teachers announced that we could all just head straight to the cafeteria instead of going to our regular classrooms.

"Come on," Pia said, heading for the door. "All that art and forgiving and stuff made me hungry!"

"Hang on." Jesse was staring across the gym. "What are Rusty and Cole doing over there?"

I looked and saw that the two boys were sweeping the floor with big brooms. They looked pretty unhappy.

"Let's go find out," I said.

We hurried over. "What's up?" Lola asked the boys. "Are you guys practicing your new super-hero identities: Super Sweeper and Broom Boy?"

"Very funny." Cole didn't laugh. "Miss Norton overheard us talking about what we did to

Stanley's sculpture. She's making us clean up the whole gym as punishment."

My friends looked kind of confused. I realized that in all the excitement, I'd forgotten to tell them about what the boys had done.

"Wait," I said. "So she caught you? What did Stanley say when he found out?"

Rusty leaned on his broom. "He was mad at first, but he forgave us," he said. "Stanley said that what we did inspired him to, like, try something new on his next great artwork or something."

Cole rolled his eyes. "Yeah. But Miss Norton didn't care that Stanley forgave us. She punished us, anyway!"

I grinned. "Serves you right," I told both boys. I wasn't surprised to hear that Stanley wasn't holding a grudge. He's a really nice kid as well as a great artist. "Have fun sweeping, you two!"

"But . . ." Jesse began, looking confused.

"I'll explain everything while we're eating," I promised. "Come on, let's go!"

Soon my friends and I were sitting around our usual table laughing over the boys' prank and their punishment. "You were right, Amy," Jesse said. "It serves them right. They need to take responsibility for what they did even if Stanley wasn't mad."

Lola sipped from her juice box and nodded. "Just like Amy and Jesse and I had to take responsibility for spilling that secret."

"And me for acting snippy with all of you," Pia added.

Maya smiled. "The important thing is that we all learned our lesson, right?" she said. "Friends sometimes make mistakes, and we have to learn to forgive one another. So from now on, we'll stay Five Best Friends forever!"

"Right," Jesse agreed. "Hey, how about what that art guy said? I can't wait to see our picture in the paper!"

I nodded. I was already looking forward to using the clipping in my next scrapbook page. "That reminds me," I said. "My mom said we could store the project in our garage when the art show is over."

"Awesome!" Lola said. "That way we can pull it out someday when we're, like, thirty or something and stick our heads through the face holes again."

I smiled. "Yeah," I agreed happily. "Because even when we're really old, like thirty or something, I know we'll still be Five Best Friends!"

Getting
Ready for the
Art Show ❀

Everyone loved my idea!

Working together in art class!

Giggles wanted to be in
Five Best Friends, too!

The Art Show

Pia and her dad at the show

Me and my parents

My awesome ribbon!

We tied for first place!

MAPLE HEIGHTS GAZETTE

Art Section

Student Art Show Dazzles!

About the Authors ♥ ❀

Kim Wayans and Kevin Knotts are actors and writers (and wife and husband) who live in Los Angeles, California. Kevin was raised on a ranch in Oklahoma, and Kim grew up in the heart of New York City. They were inspired to write the Amy Hodgepodge series by their beautiful nieces and nephews—many of whom are mixed-race children—and by the fact that when you look around the world today, it's more of a hodgepodge than ever.